Tristan's Bedtime Story

written and illustrated
by Caroline Formby

For Zoe and Simon

Child's Play (International) Limited
Swindon Lewiston Toronto Sydney Bologna

ISBN 0-85953-946-6 Printed in Singapore

It was long past Tristan's bedtime.
But the little volcano would not go to sleep.

"I want a story, I want a story,"
he repeated over and over.

"Go to sleep at once,"
his mother said.
"Or I'll tell your father."

"If you don't go to sleep,"
bellowed Tristan's father,
"you won't grow up to be
big and strong like me."

Tristan began to howl.
The louder Father Volcano
roared, the louder
Baby Tristan cried.

"Hush, little one,"
Granny's soothing voice
called across the waves.
"Promise to be quiet,
and I will tell you a story!"

Tristan stopped crying at once.
Granny's stories always
made him feel better.

All the animals gathered round
to listen, too.

"Long ago," Granny began,
"it was our job to make the world
ready for plants and animals."

Tristan closed his eyes
and tried to imagine
what the world looked like
when Granny and his parents
were young.

It wasn't easy.

"The force of our eruptions,"
Granny continued,
"made the ground shake
and the oceans boil."

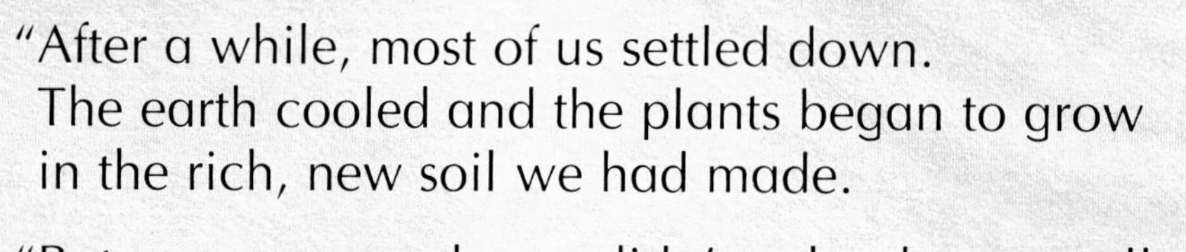

"After a while, most of us settled down.
The earth cooled and the plants began to grow
in the rich, new soil we had made.

"But one young volcano didn't calm down at all.
Can you guess who that was?"

"My Daddy," laughed Tristan.
He had heard the story before.

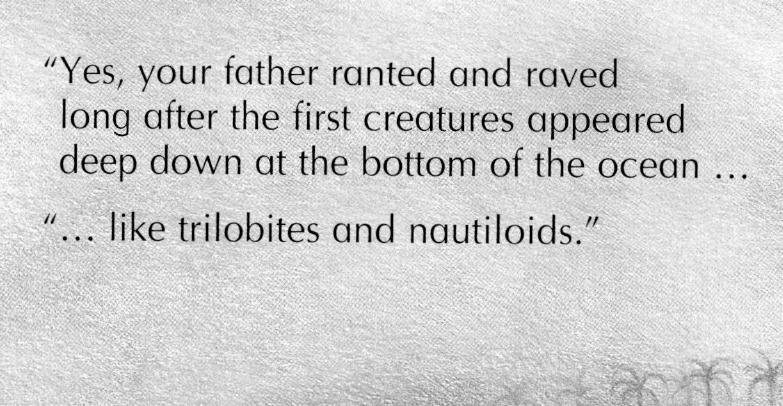

“Yes, your father ranted and raved
long after the first creatures appeared
deep down at the bottom of the ocean ...

“... like trilobites and nautiloids.”

"Eventually, some of them
crawled out of the ocean
to make a new life on land."

"Some could run very fast
and some learned to hide.
Some grew wings and learned to fly.
But they all kept well away from your father,"
Granny chuckled.

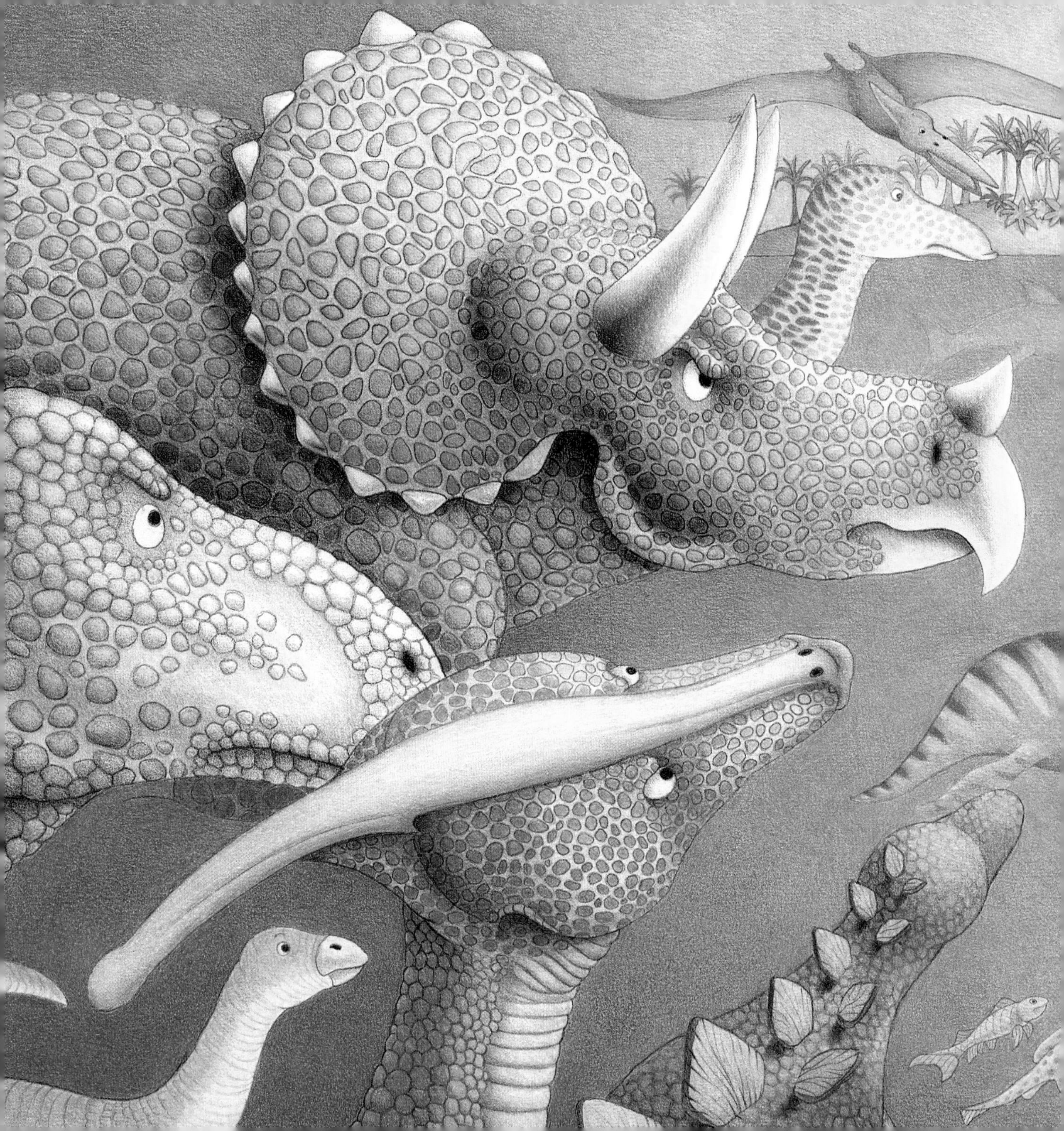

"He wasn't afraid of anything."

"Not even the dinosaurs?" asked Tristan.

"No, and they were by far the biggest animals the world has ever seen."

"They trampled the plants we had grown
and ripped up trees by their roots.
They would have destroyed everything,
but for your father!"

"When he lost his temper, they ran away
with their tails between their legs."

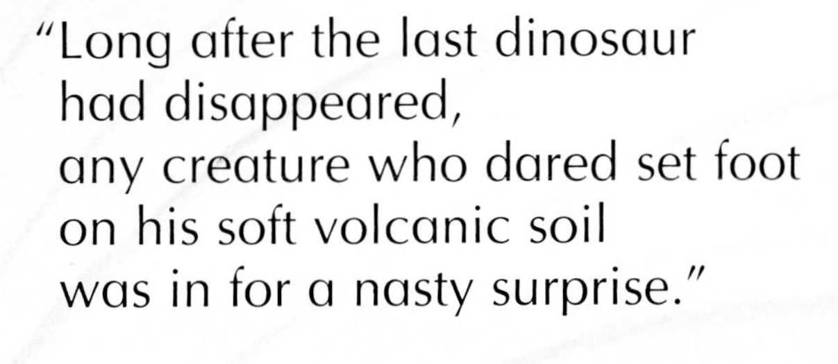

"Long after the last dinosaur
had disappeared,
any creature who dared set foot
on his soft volcanic soil
was in for a nasty surprise."

"Then, one day, something happened
that changed him for ever ...

"Do you know what that was?"

They all shook their heads.

"What could it have been?"
they asked each other.
Nobody knew the answer.

"A little baby volcano was born.
That's what made your father settle down.
And do you know who that was?"

Baby Tristan sighed happily.

He knew.

“Goodnight, Tristan,” whispered Granny.

The little volcano didn’t hear.
He was already sound asleep.